BEFRIENDING DANIEL

WHEN CHASING THE MARK GOES WRONG

E Laurel Jones

ACKNOWLEDGMENTS

This story was inspired after my husband who witnessed a squirrel chasing a cat while sitting on the porch. I would like to thank God for giving me him and my children. They are always sparking ideas that turns into a story. They never cease from encouraging me to never give up on my dreams and to always be better than the day before.

TABLE OF CONTENTS

CHAPTER 1:
JOSEPH

Joseph woke up when his face was struck by a force he had never felt before. His frontal lobe ached with pain as his head whipped back and his body spun in circles. He opened his eye to find himself hanging upside down by a rope tied to his ankles. He looked vacantly into the sneer of a stranger clenching his fists.

Where am I, and how long have I been here? Joseph thought. One of his eyes was swollen shut, and blood dripped into the other. His jaw felt like it might have been shattered.

The dim lit lights that radiated into the room revealed the decaying rats in the corner that had accumulated over the years. The holes in the sheet metal walls exposed the ducts, which were rusted and covered with layers of splattered blood. The stillness of the air combined with a strong smell of ammonia made the hairs in Joseph's nose curl.

The blood still in his body rushed to his head. He bent at the waist as much as he could then grabbed his knees to pull himself up further. His eye locked on to a pair of green eyes that peered through a large hole in the ceiling.

A group of dark, menacing-looking men approached and surrounded him, but kept their distance. Although Joseph's vision was hazy, he noticed that each of the men was wearing a ring with the same monogram that belonged to Mr. Killebrew, a nefarious businessman in town.

So, this is how my life ends, a human piñata, Joseph thought. Gravity seemed to be getting the best of him. Unable to hold his position any longer, he relaxed his body at the waist and hung upside down midair.

"Chance after chance I've given you, Joseph, and you've always somehow disappointed me," said a man from the back of the room as he sat in the back seat of his car with the door open. He struggle with himself getting out of the car. He looks down and unfasten his seatbelt. He gets out of the car, walks toward Joseph, and chokes when walking through a cloud of smoke. "What are you's, a bunch of chain smokers, here?"

Joseph immediately recognized the sound of the person's voice.

"I know, Mr. Killebrew, and I apologize, sir." Mr. Killebrew was no stranger to Joseph. He was also someone Joseph did not consider to be a friend.

"Your apologies won't make up for the millions I lost from this business deal, which YOU assured me was a good investment," snarled Mr. Killebrew.

Mr. Killebrew looked at Joseph with a tomb-like stare as he watched Joseph sway upside down. Joseph stayed silent, unsure of what he should say. Mr. Killebrew clenched his fist in apparent rage. He crushed the cigar of his top security personnel when he blew smoke in his face. "Get out a here, will ya'?"

Some of the smoke made its way to Joseph. He held his breath for as long as he could until he choked. "I'm not sure what happened! My source has always given me reliable information. She's always come through for me."

Mr. Killebrew put his hands together and crossed them at the fingers. "Well, unfortunately for you, this time wasn't the same." He separated his hands and walked closer to Joseph. The veins in his hands bulged when he made a fist.

"Mister-" started Joseph. He faltered, unable to speak as the blood continued to rush to his head. He knew it had been only a matter of time before he started to lose consciousness.

"I've had enough of listening to you. Tomorrow is my baby girl's wedding, and by the way, how do you like the haircut? Never mind. Don't answer. I promised her mother no messy business. As you know, I'd love nothing more than to finish you off, but lucky for you, my wife thinks it'll be bad luck of some sort. But when the wedding is over, we'll meet again," said Mr. Killebrew.

He nodded his head and signaled with a hand gesture to the group of men as he walked out of the light into the darkest corner of the room. The men vigorously pummeled the upper half of Joseph's body. They only stopped and stepped back when Mr. Killebrew yelled "enough."

He watched as Mr. Killebrew held a torch lit with raging flames. Joseph tried to free himself but could not reach his ankles.

"Wait! Please!" cried Joseph, fearing the worst.

Mr. Killebrew walked over to Joseph and used the torch to burn a section of the rope a few inches above Joseph's ankles. The rope split after a few seconds, and Joseph plummeted to the ground.

Covered in a cloud of dust, Joseph moaned. He placed his hand on the left side of his head to minimize the ringing in his ear. As the dust cleared, Joseph found himself alone in an abandoned warehouse. He watched as the taillights from three vehicles left him behind.

It would've been nice if someone bothered to bring my car, Joseph thought sourly. He limped toward the overgrown pasture adjacent to the highway. Joseph walked several miles holding his thumb in the air. Letting out a heavy sigh, he felt his shoulders slump. *Who am I kidding? With the way I look, even I wouldn't stop.*

A few minutes later, a car did pull off the road. The car's headlights shone on the road sign, US 17 to Savannah, 51 miles. *Great, I'm in South Carolina,* Joseph thought. He picked up speed when he got a few feet closer to the car. The passenger of the vehicle lowered the window and tossed a bottle of water to the ground as the driver quickly sped off.

Joseph struggled as he picked up the bottle. His muscles tensed and failed to relax. The cramps in his abdomen became unbearable. The bottle of water had a few pieces of ice inside that provided temporary relief when he pressed it against his bruised face.

I have to get off these streets, and quick, Joseph thought. He slowly sipped the chilled water. It gave him the strength he needed to walk the rest of the many miles home. He was thrilled when he finally saw the road sign on the freeway that read "Welcome to the City of Savannah."

I need to hurry home and get off these streets for a few days before Mr. Killebrew or his men see me.

CHAPTER 2:
DANIEL

Daniel was finally graduating from Savannah State University. He stood in line at the back of the Tiger Arena and waited to be signaled to start walking. *I thought his day would never come!* Daniel shifted his graduation cap slightly to the right as he walked to his seat.

The program ran smoothly, but more importantly for Daniel, both his parents were sitting in the audience. He knew his mother, Carol, was going to be there, but his father, George, unexpectedly had to go out of town for business. While George booked an early flight to return home, the departure time kept getting delayed. This went on for several days. No one had been sure if George was going to make it in time, but he drove straight from the airport at the maximum legal speed limit allowed to make sure he could see Daniel walk across the stage.

Carol had recently purchased a camera and had trouble remembering how to use it. She meant to take pictures of Daniel but accidentally ended up taking a few pictures of herself. George was also not very good at taking pictures either, but he managed to get a few in of Daniel for himself, and just at the right moments. It was a proud day for everyone in attendance at the graduation. Especially for Daniel and his family, as there was much to be celebrated.

After the ceremony ended, Daniel picked up his diploma from a table stationed in the back. He headed down the hall and exited through the double doors that led to the parking lot. He and his friends along with the rest of the graduating class loudly chanted, "We made it!" When the chanting subsided, some graduates walked to their cars as others waited for their rides. Daniel spotted his parents approaching. He said goodbye to his friends then walked off to meet them.

Carol incessantly waved at Daniel before she greeted him with a lingering hug and kiss, smearing her lipstick and tears all over his cheek. She held him so tightly he could hardly breathe.

George was talking on his phone. He ended the call with the person on the other end. He placed his phone inside his jacket pocket then addressed his family. "Give me MY diploma!" said George.

"What?" asked Daniel. A frown formed on his forehead as he looked at his mother.

"You heard me," said George. He looked at Daniel with an intense, sharp stare.

Daniel quickly handed the folder to his father. "Don't you mean, give me YOUR diploma?"

"Don't mess with me, son. I've worked hard for this," said George. He gripped the cover of the diploma as he held it in the air to admire it.

"I did too, remember? I was there. I sat in the classrooms and did all the work," said Daniel.

"Who was that on the phone?" asked Carol. She pulled a moist towelette from her purse.

"That was the realtor, Mike," said George. He stood tall and turned to Daniel. "Great news, son. We just sold the house."

"Isn't that wonderful news, Danny?" asked Carol as she smeared the lipstick further across Daniel's cheek to his ear as she tried to wipe it off.

In that moment Daniel wanted to celebrate with them, but fear of what the sale of the only house he'd lived in all his life meant for him gripped in the pit of his gut. *What am I going to do? I'm only twenty-three. Where am I going to live? How am I going to take care of myself?* He hugged his parents. "Congratulations Mom and Dad. You two can finally travel like you've always wanted."

"Yes, and we must be out of the house in sixty days," said George. He tapped his watch. "So, time is ticking."

"Sixty days? So soon? I didn't even know we were selling the house," said Daniel. He held his breath then used a technique he had learned as a child to regain control of his breathing. He repeatedly inhaled deeply into his nose and exhaled with force through his mouth. He did not want to panic in front of his mother and especially not in front of his father.

"We didn't sell the house. Your mother and I did. We didn't think we needed to include you in the discussion. Sixty days is enough time for you to find a place. You should have plenty of money saved up from your job, right?" asked George. He raised his brows and lowered his head. He knew he could have told his son about the sale of their home sooner but wanted to give Daniel the nudge he needed to finally leave the nest and provide for himself.

"Right. Sixty days. I should find a place well before then," answered Daniel.

"And if you need help, you know you can always come to me," said Carol. She tried to hold back her tears of joy. Daniel was not surprised she made that statement, because she had said it many times before.

Daniel smiled through the pain that had formed in his chest to put his parents at ease and resisted the overwhelming urge to fall to the ground and fold into a fetal position. "Let's go. I'm hungry." He placed each hand on his Mom and Dad's back and led them to the car. "We have to hurry to the restaurant before it gets crowded."

At the restaurant, Daniel barely touched his food. He tried to chat normally with his parents but his mind was clouded with thoughts about where he was going live.

When he got home, he immediately went to his laptop to start searching for available apartments. There wasn't much. He found a place across town that was not ideal for what he had in mind. The apartment was located on the West side of Savannah; about a thirty to forty-five-minute walk from downtown, the heart of the city. It had an extra room, but the rent was twice the amount than what was in his budget working at Let's Talk Cellular as a Senior Sales Associate in the Oglethorpe Mall. After he applied for the apartment, he shut the laptop then laid back on the bed until he fell asleep.

The next day, Daniel was awakened by an alert on his phone. The alert was a text that read his application was accepted. *Wow! That was quick.* The text informed him he had forty-eight hours to schedule a walk through with the owner of the building, Chad Wilkins, and pay the deposit if he wanted to hold the apartment. He immediately called and scheduled the appointment. After Daniel hung up the phone, his palms became sweaty and his heart fluttered. "My first apartment viewing. I think I'll take my Mom. Yes, I'll take her, that way she could help me if anything goes wrong. Plus, she has a car and I wouldn't have to wait for the bus."

Daniel went to his parents' room to tell them the good news. With a smile on his face, he turned to his dad. "I have an appointment to view an apartment tomorrow."

"So basically what you're saying is you still don't have a place to live," said George. He turned off the television and lowered his head as he looked at Daniel.

"Well, no. I guess not. But I have an appointment," said Daniel, his spirits deflating.

"And so may one hundred other people. An appointment is good, but remember you have less than sixty days to know for sure," said George.

I hope this is not what an adult feels like because I sure am clueless, Daniel thought as he left the room. He went to the living room and sat on the sofa. He looked through his phone for other available apartments in case someone else paid Chad the deposit before he could.

"Get up off that sofa. We got work to do," said Carol. She hit the top of his shoe with a long wooden stick.

Carol had rearranged her schedule for the entire day to coach Daniel for the meeting with Chad. She even downloaded a few articles from online about facial expressions and body language. After repeatedly making Daniel practice how to stand with the correct posture, using the perfect tone when speaking, and the countless number of times she whacked him with the stick, she put down her phone and raised her head as she arched her back. "Daniel, I think we got this."

"I think I need to call social services," said Daniel grumpily.

The following day, Daniel and Carol arrived outside of the apartment building thirty minutes before they were scheduled to arrive. They waited in Carol's red, 2016 Ford Fiesta SE Sedan until Chad arrived. Daniel started to feel overwhelmed when he thought about living on his own and having to make decisions for himself. To remain calm, he turned the music up and focused on his breathing.

"Alright, Danny. I want you to remember everything I taught you." Carol looked in the mirror to make sure there was no lipstick on her teeth.

In the apartment, as Daniel walked around his eyes widened, his cheeks flushed, and his heart raced. He had forgotten everything his mother taught him on how to maintain a 'poker face.' The kitchen was rather small but what Daniel liked most was the master bedroom had its own bathroom.

Carol walked around the apartment and saw chipped paint, a few missing doorknobs, spider webs, and tiles that needed to be replaced. She clutched tightly to her blouse as she looked out the living room window making sure her car was still outside. She grabbed the keys from her purse, and turned to Daniel. "Um, Danny." She stopped speaking because at that point it was too late. Daniel had signed the lease and was holding the keys to the front door in his hands. He had the biggest smile on his face, one Carol had never seen before.

"Congratulations Daniel," said Chad. He quickly stuffed the signed lease in his briefcase and headed to the front door. "Technically, your lease doesn't start until next month, but you can start moving your things in right away if you want."

"Cool. That'll give me more time to move my things out of my parents' house," said Daniel.

"Thanks for renting the place. If you have any questions or need work done around the apartment you have my number." Chad waved and shut the door before Daniel or Carol could respond. It was not long before the screeching sound of tires against the pavement as the engine roared was heard through the shut windows.

"I hope you know what you're getting into," said Carol. She tried to sound confident but her voice shook as she touched her face. She was cautious to make sure she did not touch anything as she left the apartment.

"It'll be fine, Mom," said Daniel. He placed his left hand on her shoulder as he followed her out the front door. "Don't worry. I'll be just fine. Once I clean the place up it'll be good as, well, good. It'll be good." Daniel's smile faded as he turned his back to Carol to lock the door. Carol's worrisome demeanor made him doubt the first decision he ever made in his life on his own.

CHAPTER 3:
THE MEET

The night spawned into a new day. As the sun rose, its bright light slowly crept into the apartment and flooded the bedroom. The muffled sound of the alarm made its way under the bedding where Daniel rested comfortably in his favorite spot on his worn mattress.

I have to get used to waking up in my own place. "My own place. I like the sound of that," said Daniel. He grunted as he removed the sheets from over his head and wiped the crust from the corners of his eyes.

He stumbled across the room with his eyes shut and walked into unpacked boxes as he made his way to the bathroom. After leaving the bathroom, he picked up his phone from off the dresser and went to the kitchen. He sat at the table to eat breakfast. As he looked out the window, he observed his neighbor, Mr. Holbrooke, grunt at the other neighbors for greeting him on his way back into the house.

Daniel picked up his phone and read an email his mother sent him. The subject line read: *Thinking of you, Mom.*

The body of the message contained a list of what she considered to be suitable career choices. He looked in the mirror then shook his head after reading one of the careers his mother had written down, Model.

He closed the email, sat the phone on the table, and continued eating his breakfast. When he was finished he placed the dirty dishes in the sink. He meandered back to the bedroom, straight to the closet. Finding the right outfit was easy considering the small selection he had to choose from. He polished his nametag before he pinned it to his shirt.

Daniel straightened his blue bowtie with white dots he'd fastened around the collar of his pinstriped buttoned-up shirt. He looked at the bedroom door and visualized his mother standing there, saying, "Aren't you just a handsome guy," as she would every morning after he got dressed.

Charlie, Daniel's ruggedly handsome and heavily-tattooed roommate, came from out of the other bedroom and stood in Daniel's bedroom doorway. Charlie was eating frosted corn flakes with chocolate milk from a 1.5-quart stainless-steel saucepan. He loudly slurped the milk from the spoon.

Daniel thought back to the first day he met his roommate and smirked. It was just after 10 pm, two weeks after he had moved in. He answered a knock at the door. Charlie was winded, his hair was damped sticking to his face, and his t-shirt was ruffled around the collar with tiny holes. Charlie had a large haversack over his shoulder that looked like it was going to burst at the seams. Daniel ducked his head and used his hand as a shield when Charlie had reached into his leather jacket.

"I'm here about the room you advertised," said Charlie as he pulled back his hand. Daniel was relieved to see Charlie had a sheet of paper in his hand and not some weapon. Daniel had been about to say the room had already been taken when Charlie had whipped out a wad of cash. "I can give you six months in advance." Daniel was happy someone answered the ad he posted before the money he saved depleted. He immediately took the money and showed Charlie to his room.

Daniel's absentmindedness was interrupted by the noise Charlie had been making while he ate. He chuckled. "That's an interesting meal of choice," said Daniel to break the awkward silence.

"Where are you going dressed like that, and why?" asked Charlie with a mouth full of mashed-up food.

"I am going to work," said Daniel. He missed the sarcasm in Charlie's question and didn't notice the intended insult toward his choice of wardrobe attire.

"I know," said Charlie. He smirked with a mouth full of cereal. He drooled milk down one side of his mouth. "But dressed like that?"

"Yes, Charlie. It's called professional attire. You should try it sometimes," said Daniel as he grabbed his keys and cell phone before walking out of the bedroom.

"I'll pass," said Charlie on the way back to his own bedroom.

"Whelp, if you ever change your mind-?" Daniel responded with a high-pitched tone to mask his having finally picked up on the sarcasm.

"I won't," yelled Charlie before Daniel had finished speaking. He shut his room door with his foot.

Daniel grabbed his jacket from off the coat rack and rushed out the front door to catch the bus to work.

Exiting the city bus, Daniel casually sauntered into the Oglethorpe Mall using the sliding doors that led directly to the food court. He became distracted by a crowd of patrons staring at a lightning -blue, 2018 Ford Escape SUV parked to the right, over on the far end in the corner. Adjacent to the car was a decorative stage with flashing lights, a large monitor, and a microphone. Next to the stage was a short, petite woman with freckles selling raffle tickets.

The woman selling the raffle tickets looked at Daniel with a gentle smile. Encouraged by her expression and drawn to its warmth, Daniel decided to head towards her.

"Hello," said Daniel as he shook the woman's hand. "Nice car. I don't remember seeing it here yesterday when I left to go home.

"No, you wouldn't have. It was delivered this morning," said the woman. She quietly chuckled.

"My name is Daniel, by the way."

"Hi. I'm Candace. I'm a part of a nonprofit organization, United Through Education. We collaborated with Ford to raise money to support education worldwide."

"Now that's some sauce full of awesomeness." *Sauce full…awesomeness…I can't believe I just put those words together in the same sentence,* Daniel thought. He attempted to cover his nervousness with an awkward smile.

"It sure is. Would you be interested in purchasing a raffle ticket?" asked Candace.

"It's a nice car, but I can't. When I was in grade school my always said gambling was a sickness that only trouble followed after she caught my friends and I gambling. Can I just donate the money instead?" asked Daniel.

"I would love to take your donation, but because of our partnership with Ford, you have to purchase a ticket," said Carol. She held the ticket at Daniel's eye level to entice him.

Daniel paused with uncertainty. Every hair on his body raised alerting him he was about to do something bad, something he had never done before. He was about to disobey his mother. Before he realized what he had done he already handed Candace a five-dollar bill. *It's just one ticket. How much harm could it do?*

Daniel had been about to respond to Candace when she had asked if he thought the car looked beautiful. He did not because he became distracted by a woman with brunette-colored hair at the other end of the food court. She was tall, lean, and the lower half of her dress floated around her thighs showcasing her long, luscious legs. Daniel glanced at his watch.

"Whoa! Look at the time. Gotta go," said Daniel. He shoved the raffle ticket into his front pocket revealing the ticket numbers. Daniel offered a distracted smile to Candace before he hurried off to work.

Daniel entered Let's Talk Cellular, reorganizing the brochures on the counter on his way to clock in. He focused his eyes on the banners to ensure he properly positioned them. He accidentally bumped into the tall, brunette woman from the food court causing the folder in her hand to fall to the floor.

"Karen," said Daniel as he squatted to collect the papers and the folder the papers fell from. He became mesmerized by the woman's legs. He cleared his throat. "God, I'm such a klutz. I'm so sorry."

"Don't worry about it," said Karen. She was also an employee of Let's Talk Cellular but had only been working there for a couple of weeks. Daniel fell in love with her the first time he had seen her but had not yet developed the courage to ask her to join him for dinner and a show. Karen laughed placing one hand on his shoulder as she took the folder. "Thank you," she blushed, walking off to converse with another coworker.

Daniel subtly watched before going over to his workstation to begin his shift.

"Here! Here!" announced a woman with big hair as she loudly popped bubble gum. When Daniel looked up he saw it was Suzanne.

She handed each associate a sheet of paper without waiting for them to take hold of it.

Daniel was taken back when she shoved the sheet of paper in his face. "Thank you, Suzanne. How are-"

"Yeah, yeah, whatever!" said Suzanne. She continued to pass out the rest of the papers to the other coworkers before making her way to the back office.

As Daniel read the paper, his heart raced faster, and his jaw dropped. This was everything he had been waiting for. The paper was an announcement for an opening in management, inviting all interested parties to apply. Anticipating this moment, Daniel looked through the top drawer of his workstation and pulled out his resume.

"I know you're in here," said Daniel, quietly told himself. "Here you go," he smiled, finding his pre-printed resume at last. He carefully looked it over, making sure there were not any stains or wrinkles on the paper before taking it to Suzanne.

In the hallway outside of Suzanne's office, Daniel became motionless. His heart pounded. He heavily breathed as he thought of Suzanne. She intimidated him by the way she would stare with an evil-eye, never moving, as if she was frozen in time. Suzanne had been working at the company for the past three years. Her position was quite confusing because all she did was loudly chew gum while stapling the same sheet of paper over and over. Daniel gathered the strength he needed to enter the office although he was wracked with nervousness as he walked through the door.

"What do you want?" shouted Suzanne without making eye contact.

"To turn in my resume," stuttered Daniel. He suspected that Suzanne knew how nervous she made him feel and that she found it amusing.

"I'm supposed to ask what makes you think you're a good fit for the position." Suzanne stopped stapling the paper and looked at Daniel. "Make it quick."

"Well, I think I'm perfect for the position because I've been planning on applying for it for months and-"

"Good enough. Put your resume over there," snapped Suzanne. She pointed to her right with the stapler. "I'll get to it whenever I get to it."

Daniel saw that the table was completely covered and stacked with papers and folders. He discretely placed his resume in the tray on the desk labeled Important Papers, then quickly left the office.

"You got this. Just stay calm," said Daniel. He repeated those words to motivate himself on his way back to his workstation.

Two hours into his shift he took a ten-minute break. As he walked into the employees' break room he observed his coworkers. John was on his phone as he was making a cup of coffee and Sharon, Michelle, and Audrie whispered as they were huddled in the corner. The women immediately stopped speaking to each other and left the break room when Daniel entered. Audrie closed the door behind her but it had sprung open again.

Daniel approached Mr. Jameson. He was one of the managers. Mr. Jameson sat at the same table in the back of the room reading a newspaper that was always two days old. He treated the table as if it was his own private territory. If anyone else sat at the table he would stare at the person until they moved.

"Hello, Mr. Jameson," said Daniel. He wiped his sweaty palms on the front of his pants.

Mr. Jameson glanced up at Daniel and relaxed all of his facial and body muscles, making it different for Daniel to read his body language to know what he may have been thinking.

"I hope I'm not disturbing you," said Daniel. He knew that he was, but did not want to come off as being someone who was not considerate. "May I have a moment of your time?"

"Yes," said Mr. Jameson. He closed the newspaper and used his index finger to not lose the page he was reading.

"It's about the management position," continued Daniel. A stiffening chill took over Daniel's body as he stared into Mr. Jameson's cold eyes. Daniel started to look away, then gathered his courage and stood tall, and faced Mr. Jameson squarely. "What do you think are the chances of corporate selecting me for the management position?"

"Percentages, of you, as a manager," said Mr. Jameson. He kept his deadpan stare, placed the newspaper on his lap, then snorted while he jarringly laughed. "Zero. I mean, look at you. You are a hard worker, yes, but a manager? No." Mr. Jameson snickered and went back to reading his newspaper.

"I see. Thank you," said Daniel. At that moment Daniel felt as if he had lost all hope. He forcibly held back his inner emotions as his shoulders drooped.

John overheard the conversation and cackled as he left the room. Daniel went back to his workstation. He suspected everyone was gossiping about him because of the way they looked away when he had looked at him. Karen confirmed his suspicions when she looked at him, lowered her eyebrows, and frowned. Daniel bolted out of the store when everyone's laughter grew louder. Karen chased after him.

Daniel heard Karen calling for him, but he couldn't face her. He kept running until he was lost in the crowd. He stopped, sagged against the wall, and gasped for air. He looked at his reflection through the store's window. *I think it is time for a make-over.*

He entered a nearby shoe store. He was taken aback by the wall-to-wall collection of designer shoes. He walked backwards toward the door and caused quite a scene when he knocked over a few boxes and a billboard.

The alarm on his phone went off alerting him his break was over. He trudged back to work and avoided meeting his coworkers' eyes for the rest of the day. When his shift ended, he immediately went home.

Later that night in his apartment, Daniel rummaged through the refrigerator, grabbing a container of mint chocolate ice cream that was in the back of the freezer. He slung the door closed on his way to the pantry. He grabbed a bag of chips and tucked it under his arms along with an Almond Joy candy bar.

Before leaving the kitchen, he went back to the refrigerator and grabbed a bottle of soda. He headed to his bedroom where he hid to eat.

"I totally overdid it," groaned Daniel. His stomach rumbled as he took the remaining snacks back to the kitchen.

Charlie walked into the kitchen wearing a buttoned-up collared shirt with dark blue jeans. He pulled a bottle of beer from the top shelf of the refrigerator.

"You clean up nicely," said Daniel as he wiped potato crumbs from his lips. "So, what are you getting into tonight, or should I say who?"

"There's a new spot a buddy of mine wants to check out," said Charlie.

"Sounds like fun. Give me a second to grab my jacket," Daniel said, happy for any distraction. Charlie grimaced while Daniel's back was turned.

Charlie's cell phone rang with Linkin Park's "*Numb*" as the ringtone. He answered the phone and whispered, "I'll be down as soon as I ditch my roomy. Yes, I know. Okay, I'm coming down." He hung up the phone and met Daniel in the living room. "That was Benny. He had to take his girl's car tonight, and it's just too small to fit us all. Maybe next time."

"Yeah, next time," said Daniel, dejected.

The sound of a car's horn broke the awkward silence. Charlie grabbed another beer before rushing out the door. Daniel heard the commotion they were making outside and went to the window that had been left over. Benny was shouting at Charlie. Benny was in a shadow black, 2016 GT Premium Convertible Mustang. There were no other passengers in the car. Daniel could obviously have comfortably sat in the back seat.

"Hurry up before all the good parking spaces are taken," Benny yelled to Charlie.

"Chill. You know I had to ditch my roommate," said Charlie.

After Daniel listened to his stomach rumble again, he grabbed his jacket and keys and left the apartment to walk off all the food he had eaten.

Daniel's thoughts were preoccupied as he walked. Despair about his job competed with wistful longing for Karen. He imagined himself on a romantic date with her. They were eating steak while sitting at a table stationed on a cliff that overlooked the city. He leaned in to kiss her. A bright light flashed from her eyes and she made the sound of a car's horn every time she opened her mouth. *This makes no sense.* As Daniel came back to reality, he realized he was standing in the middle of the street, facing oncoming traffic.

"Hey! Look where you're going next time," yelled a taxi driver.

Daniel leaped back onto the sidewalk. "Man, that was a close one," he said, chagrined.

The taxi driver flipped Daniel off as he sped away. Daniel bent over to tie his shoelace. The raffle ticket fell from his pocket. After picking up the ticket, he looked through the window of the restaurant. His shoulders slumped and his mouth fell open when he saw Karen dining out with an unfamiliar man.

The man had his back to Daniel, so the only thing he could see was the man's watch with a distinctive scar above the wristband when he raised his hand to get the waitress' attention. And from what Daniel could observe, the man's watch was not cheap. The watch was certainly one he could never afford. He looked to his left and saw that he was in front of Ruth's Chris Steak House, a pricey, upscale restaurant located on West Bay Street. As he stared into the restaurant, he knew for sure he could not afford the watch the man was wearing, or Karen.

An unwanted image of Mr. Jameson popped into his head. Mr. Jameson was mocking Daniel as his coworkers stood by and laughed. *No Karen and no promotion.* Daniel forced the unpleasant thoughts away and marched over to a bar at the other end of the street. He took a vacant seat at the bar and indulged in the sweet nectars of 'dirty waters', Tequila with a few cubes of ice. He signaled to the bartender to bring another drink. After counting how much money he had left in his wallet he wished the liquor store was open so he could drown his sorrows in a more cost-effective way.

A man with a bushy beard entered the bar smoking a cigarette. He sat down next to Daniel and said, "Only one of two things could cause a man to drown his troubles away."

He dragged on his cigarette, exhaled the smoke, and asked, "Money or a woman. Which is it, kid?"

"Karen," answered Daniel. He gulped down the remaining liquor in his glass.

"I see. The name's Rusty."

"Daniel."

"Good name kid. So, what trouble's Karen putting you through?" asked Rusty.

Daniel rambled on for about ten minutes before he stood with wobbly knees. "Who am I ki-kid-ding? I know I don't have a chance with Cuh-Care-Ren."

"There's no such thing as not having a chance. Don't give up so easily. She'd be foolish not to give you a chance," insisted Rusty.

Daniel felt a little reassured. He decided he would head back to work an hour before his shift started to begin his makeover in hopes it would impress Karen. He paid for his drink. As he left the bar, he stumbled into a few patrons that were coming in.

The bartender walked over to Rusty and cleaned off the section of the bar where Daniel sat and asked Rusty, "You really think that kid has a chance?"

"Hell no," scoffed Rusty.

Rusty and the bartender laughed as he poured Rusty another drink. Rusty reached for his wallet to pay for the drink.

"Don't worry. This one's on the house," said the bartender.

Rusty picked up the drink. Before he could put the glass to his lips a woman snatched the glass from his hands and drained the glass with one swallow.

"You want to dance?" asked the woman.

"I'd love to," grinned Rusty as he got up from the stool.

"Be gentle," said the bartender.

"I will," replied Rusty.

"It's you who I'm worried about," said the bartender as he continued to clean off the counter before walking off to take another customer's order.

Rusty knew then he was in trouble, but it was the kind of trouble he'd hoped to find.

Daniel safely made his way back home and staggered through the door. Too intoxicated to go any further, he tossed his keys at the coffee table. The keys landed on the floor. Unable to take another step, he collapsed to the floor where he slept until the next day.

CHAPTER 4:
IMPLEMENTING THE PLAN

Joseph looked out the bedroom window of his apartment through torn blinds and ripped curtains. A black 2013 Dodge Charger with tinted windows was parked a few feet away. A hand stretched outward from the driver's side window to flick the ashes from the cigarette. The ring on the man's pinky finger revealed that the hand belonged to one of the men that worked for Mr. Killebrew.

Finding himself in a bit of a pickle, Joseph wanted to call someone for help, but there was no one he knew would answer. His treacherous ways had caused a rift in the relationship between him and his father. He looked at his Dad's name on the screen of his phone and held back his tears. "I cannot allow you to keep putting your mother and me through this. If this is the life you choose, I never want to speak to you again," were the last words his father spoke to him before he boarded the bus leaving Chicago to Georgia four years ago.

Joseph had managed to avoid Mr. Killebrew since their last encounter, but it seemed as if his time had finally run out. Joseph left the apartment before Mr. Killebrew sent his men to see if he had been inside hiding. He went up to the rooftop and jumped to the adjacent building to keep from being seen. Then he took the staircase that led to the alley a block over from where the men that worked for Mr. Killebrew had parked and hitched a ride on the back of a moving truck. *I have to come up with a quick score and hit the road before I'm history.*

Joseph hopped off the back of the truck and walked into the park then headed east before turning right on Abercorn Street. As he looked at the cars waiting at the traffic light, his heart fluttered as if it had been trying to stop beating. Mr. Killebrew was in the back seat of one of the cars on his phone yelling at the person on the other end. Joseph leaped into a nearby tall bush to keep from being seen.

"Take the side roads. I don't want to be late," Mr. Killebrew barked at his driver.

After the light turned green and Mr. Killebrew was no longer in sight, Joseph got to his feet and dusted himself off. He ran a few blocks in the opposite direction Mr. Killebrew's car was traveling. Just when Joseph had been about to relax his breathing he saw another one of Mr. Killebrew's men leaving the coffee shop and hid behind a tree until the man had left.

Joseph sat on a bench near the bus stop to rest. When he looked up, he saw the billboard to the Oglethorpe Mall off in the distance. "Now there's a place I can blend in with the crowd."

Joseph scampered into the parking lot of the Mall. His heart pounded as he dashed and ducked between vehicles. He peered through the windows of each car hoping for one of the doors to be unlocked, so he could steal anything of value. After having no such luck, he strode into the Mall and hoped his chances of lucrative pilfering might increase. He really needed a score.

Joseph watched as Candace stood near the car holding a roll of raffle tickets and a small container. He casually approached her surveying to see who had been aware of their surroundings to notice him. "Hey."

"Hi. Would you like to purchase a ticket? It's for this lovely car," smiled Candace.

"Yes, it is lovely, but unfortunately, I only have a debit card," said Joseph.

"No worries. We have a machine you can use," said Candace. She pointed toward the ATM not far from them.

"Oh, you do," said Joseph. He patted his front pockets. "Well, look at that."

"Look at what?" asked Candace.

"My wallet. It's not on me," said Joseph.

"That's not good," said Candace.

"I bet I left my wallet at home. Maybe next time I'll buy a ticket," said Joseph.

Candace started to respond but the buzzer sounded ending any new entries for the car. "Okay then. Bye!"

Joseph slowly walked past the stage, making sure to put himself between Candace and the car. As she passed, he quickly snatched a few tickets. He ripped the tickets into two and kept one-half for himself and placed the other half into the container before Candace walked behind the curtain. Joseph camouflaged himself in with the crowd.

A few minutes later, the curtains behind the stage were lowered using an automated system. Lights began to flash on the car and were synchronized to the music playing through the speakers. People began to take notice and dance as they filled the area near the stage. After a bell had rung, a professionally dressed short-haired woman walked up to the microphone.

"Hello, everyone. My name is Millie." Then she loudly announced, "Thank you all for coming." The crowd's response was muted, but she ignored the lack of cheers of joy. "Okay. The moment you've all been waiting for. Let's see who the lucky winner of this lovely new car is."

She clapped and encouraged the crowd to clap with her. Everyone remained silent.

"Come on already and say my numbers," whispered Joseph as he desperately gripped onto his tickets.

"I certainly can't wait to meet you and take a picture with you and your new car," said Millie. She smiled and giggled while she slightly swayed.

As the television monitor displayed the winning numbers Joseph watched as Millie announced them.

"1-4-9-3-3-8," said Millie.

Joseph became excited because so far all the numbers she had called out were an exact match to one of the tickets in his hand. He couldn't believe his luck.

"Okay. Here we go. The last number you all are waiting for is 2," said Millie.

Joseph moved his thumb to reveal the last number on the ticket. The number was 3. After he saw his ticket was off by one number, his stomach had sunken inward as the room began to rotate in all directions. His face turned bright red as he bit his bottom lip. He ripped the tickets into pieces and tossed the ripped tickets to the floor.

He screamed and yanked at his hair before he stretched his skin from his face. After one deep breath, he pulled himself together before he leisurely walked through the Mall. He entered NEXT Step, a designer men's shoe store, because it was crowded. While looking at a pair of Stacy Adams, Joseph became distracted by the sound of a gullible man's voice off in the distance.

"Why is this so difficult?" asked the man. He continued to complain as he heavily sighed while sinking his chin into his chest. "They're only shoes." The man grunted and his rants became more aggressive.

The other customers cleared a path. The man who caught Joseph's attention was Daniel. Joseph had been about to turn away until he noticed the raffle ticket in Daniel's pocket. Joseph's piercing eyes immediately fixated onto the winning numbers. He bit into his fist to contain his emotions.

"How's it going?" asked Joseph. He nodded his head and pointed to the shoe Daniel had been holding.

"Worse than it looks," said Daniel. He sighed heavily.

"I did notice you having a bit of trouble there," said Joseph. He waited but Daniel did not respond. "I hate picking out shoes too, but we do have to wear them."

"Yes, we do," said Daniel. He placed the shoes on the rack before taking a few steps to the side, away from Joseph.

"I'd like to meet the genius that said your clothes and shoes are what defines you because they don't," said Daniel as he walked to the other side of the store.

"But the ladies, they do love them," said Joseph as he followed Daniel.

"Have you made up your mind on which pair of shoes you're getting?" asked Joseph.

"Umm. No, but you probably have other things to worry about," answered Daniel.

"No, I'd love to help. Trust me," said Joseph with a crooked smile.

Daniel looked at his watch again. "I don't know. I only have about fifteen more minutes before my shift starts."

"This won't take long. Trust me," said Joseph. Every second he stood near Daniel he found it more difficult to keep his eyes off the ticket.

Daniel gave in and let Joseph know he was looking for a pair of shoes that was more of a style that a manage would wear. Joseph sadly informed him that neither of the shoes in that area projects the appearance of a manager.

The sales associate walked over to Daniel and Joseph and asked, "Have either of you decided on which pair of shoes you'll be getting today?"

Daniel did not answer. It seemed something had caught his attention from outside the store. Daniel stared through the glass window as if he was frozen in time.

"My friend, Daniel, and I are going to need a few more minutes," said Joseph.

Daniel's forehead wrinkled and his eyes scrunched together. *Friends? We just met!* He frowned at Joseph but quickly adjusted his face and turned his back to Joseph.

Joseph realized he must do or say something quickly before his window of opportunity disappeared. "Oh, silly me. I'm always getting ahead of myself. My name is Joseph."

Daniel placed the shoe back on the rack. "It happens to the best of us. My name is Daniel."

Joseph grabbed a different pair of shoes off the shoe rack that was neither professional or screamed 'I am a manager.' He handed the pair of shoes to Daniel while staring at the raffle ticket. *Fall. Please drop.* Joseph forced himself to take his eyes off the ticket. "Here, you should buy these if you're trying to make the statement 'I am on my way to the top'."

However, Daniel was not an easy person to convince.

"And I bet the next time you wear these shoes you will definitely be noticed," added Joseph to close the sale.

Daniel thought back to the man Karen was dining with at the restaurant and responded, "It is going to take more than a new pair of shoes considering what I'm up against."

"Trust me. Someone will compliment you on your new style. And if not, I have a coupon ticket for a meal, so lunch will be on me. And if no one says anything about the shoes you can give me whatever ticket or anything you may have on you," said Joseph.

"All right then. What do I have to lose?" asked Daniel. He thought the odds were easily stacked in his favor because all of his college friends teased him how he dressed.

After purchasing the shoes, Daniel thanked Joseph for his help and left the store unaware of Joseph tailing him.

Unbeknownst to Joseph, Daniel was on his way back to work. Luckily for him, there was a lounge area where he sat and hid behind a standing billboard ad and watched Daniel without being recognized.

Joseph wilted in the chair as the seconds turned into minutes. He struggled to keep his eyelids open. A beam of light flickered into Joseph's eyes making it difficult for him to see. After regaining his focus, he saw that the light flickering in his eyes was the light reflecting from off a woman's diamond necklace that was loosely hanging from the back of her blouse as she stood in line at the coffee shop.

Joseph stood in line behind her. He pulled all the money he had from his front pocket to count it. Joseph became nervous. He only had a few dollars to last him for the rest of the week. He was relieved when he saw a sign indicating that the price of a cup of coffee had been discounted to celebrate the store's tenth year of opening. And even better, there were free refills.

He took a step forward closer to the woman and observed the other patrons and their vulnerability to theft. Looking to his left, he saw a man putting cream and sugar in his coffee with new crisp fifty-dollar bills sticking out of his back pocket. Looking to his right, he saw a blouse hanging from a woman's bag and a cell phone sticking out of the diaper bag being carried by the woman she was speaking with.

Looking forward, he stealthily reached for the woman's necklace. He gracefully glided his hands through her hair. The tip of his fingers touched the back of her collar. *Almost there!...*

"Next," shouted the cashier.

The woman stepped forward, causing Joseph to miss his opportunity to snatch the necklace. Joseph waited his turn and approached the counter before being called.

"Welcome to the Coffee Shop. How may I make this experience a pleasurable one for you?" smiled the cashier.

"Yes, I'll have a large coffee," said Joseph. He placed the loose change he pulled from his pockets onto the counter until he had just enough to pay for the coffee.

He grabbed a handful of sugar packets on his way back to the lounge area where he waited for Daniel to finish his shift.

As the minutes rolled into hours, and after his sixth refill of coffee, he went back for his seventh refill.

Standing in line: him and the cashier have a serious stare down.

"I'll have another cup, please," said Joseph.

"We're out," said the cashier as she squinted her eyes.

"But you have a freshly brewed pot right there," said Joseph.

The cashier ground her teeth and clenched her jaws in frustration. "You're correct sir. But this pot is for paying customers only."

To Joseph's dismay, the sign next to the coffee pot read *For Paying Customers Only* next to the empty coffee pot that read *Free Refills*.

He hovered over the counter and squirmed in his pants. "May I use the restroom?"

"Yes, you may," answered the cashier.

"Thank you," said Joseph.

"It's down the hall to the right," said the cashier. She pointed to her left.

Joseph glanced at Daniel before scurrying off to the restroom. He flushed the toilet, ran out of the restroom without washing his hands, and returned to the lounging area.

When he arrived, Daniel was no longer at his workstation. It was a female associate helping a customer. He grabbed a fist full of his hair and screamed, "No!" In a frenzy, he bolted into the store Daniel worked and threw himself onto the counter.

"Welcome-"

"Where's the guy that was here just a few minutes ago?" demanded Joseph as he grabbed her by the arm.

She pulled back and looked at the manager who was talking on his personal phone. "His shift ended. Is there something I could help you with?" she asked.

"No! He was such a great help when he was helping me with my Grandmother. She had to go to the restroom. Is there any way you could give me his number?" asked Joseph, perspiring.

"No, I can't. It goes against company policy," she answered firmly.

"Right. Company policy," said Joseph.

Feeling defeated for the day, Joseph left the Mall. He stood at the curbside with his head down as he waited for the bus to drive by. "Great. There goes my ride." Then at the last second, Joseph looked up and saw Daniel on the bus sitting by himself holding in his possession something that appeared to be similar in shape and color as the raffle ticket he purchased earlier. It was only logical that Daniel was holding the raffle ticket. "He still doesn't know he has the winning ticket," Joseph said with a cunning smile, but he had to make sure. He just did not know how he was going to do it without being noticed.

Later that night after sneaking back into his apartment, Joseph glanced out the window to see if Mr. Killebrew still had a few of his men parked out front. He was relieved when he saw no cars were parked out front, but looked out all the windows in his apartment to make sure they had not parked anywhere else. "Good. They're gone, for now. Man, I got to get my hands on that ticket. I can sell the car and finally get out of this dump."

He pulled out a coin from his front pocket and flipped it as he paced back and forth. He did this to help him stay focused while thinking. "How can I approach Daniel tomorrow without looking too suspicious?" he repeatedly asked himself.

Not paying attention to where he stepped, Joseph banged his right foot into one of the dumbbells he'd left in the middle of the floor. "I got it. I know how I'm going to get my hands on that ticket," he said in excruciating pain as he held his hurt foot while he hopped on the other. He rejoiced thinking of what it was that caught Daniel's attention when he was staring through the glass window of the store.

His joy quickly turned to sadness when he stepped down on his right foot on his way to the bedroom. There he peacefully slumbered dreaming of himself driving down the highway in a car made of money.

CHAPTER 5:

THE HUNT

Joseph left the apartment using the fire escape that led to the alley adjacent to his apartment building. He frightened away two cats that were fighting on the hood of his car before attaching the spark plugs and battery cables. In a hurry, he slammed the hood of the car too hard, and the driver's side view mirror popped out.

"Great," grumbled Joseph in a sarcastic tone while he rolled down the window. He then reattached the side mirror using duct tape to hold it in place. "The plan is going to work," he repeated to himself as he drove off trying to stay optimistic about his plans for the day.

Joseph arrived at the Mall and sat in his rusted 1987 Monte Carlo waiting for the stores to open. The car's dented rear bumper and missing trunk door did not make it a prize seller, but it got him where he needed to go. The car backfired when he turned the engine off, as it usually did. People who were passing on foot ducked for cover, thinking an active shooter was nearby. He looked at his watch. 8:31, still almost thirty minutes before the Mall opened. "You got the whole day to get this right. Don't mess this one up." Joseph choked on a dark cloud of smoke when he exited the car.

The security guard slowly approached the door talking on his cell phone. Joseph got out of his car and walked toward the Mall. Just as he approached the door, Joseph read his nametag. "Good morning officer Miles," said Joseph after he opened the door.

Officer Miles nodded his head as he slowly sipped his coffee.

A few minutes later Daniel's bus arrived. Joseph sat at the table next to the billboard displaying the winning numbers of the raffle ticket.

When Daniel entered the Mall, Joseph, hiding his face, used his body to block the view of the winning numbers as Daniel walked past the sign.

After a few hours of working, Daniel's alarm on his phone went off alerting him it was time for his lunch break. He handed his last customer their bag while tirelessly smiling. "Thank you and please come again!" On his way out, Karen stood in his path.

"Hello," said Karen as she played with her hair.

Daniel could tell something was bothering her, but he did not pry hoping it had nothing to do with yesterday. "Hello, Karen."

With droopy eyes, she pursed her lips together in a downward smile. "Daniel, about yesterday-"

"Don't worry about it," said Daniel to avoid the topic. He did not want to relive that embarrassing moment.

Karen glanced around as she searched for words to say. She blushingly smiled looking downward. "I see you went shopping." Karen tucked her hair behind her ears.

"Trying something new," said Daniel.

"Well, I like them," said Karen.

"You do?" said Daniel suspiciously. He was caught off guard. Daniel was always used to being made fun of for the way he dressed.

"Yes. They are different," said Karen as she looked over Daniel's shoulder. "Got to go. Mr. Jameson is coming." She gave him a smile, then scurried off.

"Daniel, good, you're still here," said Mr. Jameson as he looked at his clipboard. "Hurry back. I'm expecting a high flow of customers today and need everyone available."

Daniel's heart pounded, his knees slightly wobbled, and his palms moistened with sweat leaving the store from interacting with Karen.

Joseph quickly treaded up to Daniel and accidentally collided into him on purpose. "Excuse me. I am so sorry."

"Hey, you," said Joseph after he made eye contact with Daniel. He pretended as if he was shocked to see Daniel. "Joseph, from the other day in the shoe store."

"Yeah. Right! You wouldn't believe what just happened to me," said Daniel.

Joseph tried desperately to listen, but his focus became distracted as he looked Daniel over searching for signs of the ticket. Re-focusing himself on Daniel, he only heard the last few words.

"I can't believe it. Karen liked my shoes," said Daniel.

"I told you she would," said Joseph, masking his emotions with a smile. He did not want to show how baffled he really was.

"Yes, you did, I think," said Daniel. He tried to draw a memory, but his thoughts were blank.

"She's all you talked about," said Joseph to quickly distract him.

"I sure hope that's all I did last night," said Daniel. He rubbed his forehead and slid his hand down to his jaw while he shook his head. "Well, I am a man of my word."

"Yes, I knew you were," said Joseph as he cunningly smiled.

Daniel pulled out a ticket from his jacket pocket and handed it to Joseph. "Here you go. As we agreed. Sorry, it's not much." He handed Joseph a ticket with the front facing downward.

Joseph became filled with excitement. He took the ticket and flipped it over. The muscles in his face tightened as he struggled to smile when he realized the ticket was a coupon for a free meal and Daniel was wearing a different jacket from the day before.

"Looks like lunch is on me," said Daniel before he walked off.

He must have placed the ticket in another pocket, but where? Joseph thought. He scurried up to Daniel and lamely asked about the restaurant's food and service. It was all he could think of.

"Oh, they're great, and the selection of food and drinks is quite tasteful," said Daniel.

"I definitely will give them a try," said Joseph.

Daniel walked off. Joseph fell a few steps behind as Daniel entered a nearby store. In the restaurant, Daniel ordered his food and sat down.

"Man, this place isn't bad after all," said Joseph as he sat down at the table with Daniel without his permission. "Nice place. I see why you come here a lot. So, when are you going to ask her out?"

Daniel choked on air. He was startled by Joseph's presence. "Who?" asked Daniel as he tried to clear his throat.

"Karen," replied Joseph. He rolled his eyes as he picked up the silverware that was rolled inside a napkin.

"Don't get me wrong. I do want to ask her out but let's be realistic, look at me," said Daniel.

"I'm looking, and what's wrong with you?" asked Joseph even though he knew the answer.

"For one, it's going to take more than shoes to get her to go on a date with me," said Daniel.

"True, but we can work on that. Just give me your address and phone number and I'll come by later," said Joseph brightly.

"Excuse me?" asked Daniel.

"To help you with Karen, put some outfits together, and maybe do some role-playing of you asking her out," said Joseph.

"Um, see, I'm not sure... I barely know you," said Daniel.

Daniel continued to speak but Joseph became distracted as a woman wearing a large diamond necklace stopped at the window to speak with someone she knew. Joseph gazed deeply at the diamonds as the lighting that bounced off of them made the diamonds sparkle.

"I'm really starting to see why you love this place," grinned Joseph.

"The food is rich."

After no response from Daniel, Joseph turned his head and saw an empty seat. He'd been so distracted that he did not even notice Daniel when he got up from the table and walked toward the exit doors of the restaurant.

"Did you see where my friend went?" Joseph asked the busboy who was cleaning the table next to his.

"Yes, he's right there," said the busboy. He pointed at Daniel. He was on the outside of the restaurant looking in.

Joseph and Daniel made eye contact. Daniel hurried off. Joseph shoved his way through the dancers and chased after him.

CHAPTER 6:
THE CHASE

Daniel bumped into a few patrons as he looked back a few times running down the walkway.

"Daniel, wait," yelled Joseph. Joseph was barely able to keep up with Daniel because of his bad feet. He stopped and leaned against the wall. "These pain meds are wearing off." He grimaced as he massaged his left foot in the palm of his right hand.

Daniel turned the corner and hid in the nearby picture booth located in the center of the aisle. Before he could close the curtain, the camera captured the hilarious reactions to him being blindsided by the light. He blinked several times to regain focus of his vision, he dropped his mouth wide open when he saw that Karen was already sitting in the booth. He immediately pulled the curtain completely closed after he looked over Karen's shoulder and saw Joseph shuffling by them.

Daniel and Karen laughed hilariously at the images in the photo.

"I'm truly sorry for ruining your pictures," said Daniel with a rueful smile. His face turned pale.

"No. I love them," said Karen.

Daniel was filled with so many emotions he did not know which one to release first. He knew he had to play it cool. "You do?" said Daniel as his voice trembled.

"I mean." Karen wrung her hands then scratched down the front of her neck. "Would you like to get something to eat?"

Daniel tried to hold back his excitement as he sat tall. It was all he could do to contain his excitement. "Yes I-I-I." He choked on his words. The words stuck in his mouth like molasses in January. He raised a hand to cover his mouth as he cleared his throat. "I'd love to."

Karen and Daniel laughed over a delightful meal in the middle section of the food court. When they finished their meal, Karen leaned into Daniel. "I honestly enjoyed myself. It's always great to take a break from work and just breathe a little, you know?"

"I do. We definitely should-" Before Daniel could finish his sentence, he saw Joseph approaching, took a sip of his drink, and quickly ran off while pretending to choke. When he turned the corner, he slowed down and glanced behind himself to make sure Joseph was not following. He let out a heavy sigh and sauntered to the other end of the hall. As he got to the other end, he halted when he saw Joseph turning the corner walking in his direction. Daniel pivoted before running into a nearby store.

Hiding behind a mannequin, he watched Joseph as he walked past the store. Seconds passed. He exited the store and ran in the opposite direction but was stopped by yellow tape construction workers put up to secure an area undergoing remodeling. Daniel decided instead of waiting until the Mall closed to take his chances, he carefully walked in the direction Joseph had gone, hoping to not get caught.

A few feet away Daniel saw a clown pushing a cart. He walked next to the cart and hid behind the balloons attached to the clown's cart. He and the clown were stopped by a teacher and her students who were on a field trip. The students purchased some of the balloons and other items before entering a nearby store.

A group of girls' voices loudly screeched as they ran past Daniel, pointing to a sign in the window of a clothing store promoting its sale of fifty percent off on all items. Hearing the commotion, Joseph's curiosity caused him to turn around.

"Oh no," said Daniel. He wailed in a frenzy.

The two made eye contact and stared at each other like a deer caught in headlights. Daniel forced his way through a large crowd and bumped into a tiny man dressed in all white. The man tumbled into a cotton candy machine.

Joseph made his way through the crowd. A man spinning in circles inside of the cotton candy machine caught his attention. His vision blurred. He shook his head to regain focus and continued his chase.

Over on the other side of the Mall in the food court, Karen checked her watch then stood up from the table. Daniel walked up from behind and tapped her on the shoulder.

"There you are," said Daniel as if nothing had happened.

"Daniel, are you, all right? You gave me quite the scare," said Karen.

He patted her back. "I'm fine. Really, I am. Look at the time. We should be getting back to work."

"Oh, my appointment. I almost forgot. I can't miss it," said Karen.

"Go, hurry," insisted Daniel.

Without thinking, Karen kissed him on the cheek. She scurried off blushing when realizing what she'd done.

Daniel saw Joseph walking his way and hid in a large toy castle in the children's playing area. There he bumped into a young boy.

"Stranger danger, stranger danger," shouted the kid.

"Hush. Be quiet," whispered Daniel furiously.

Two angry parents marched their way over to the toy castle.

"Oh no, you don't. I know you're not trying to touch my child," said one of the parents. She grabbed Daniel by the collar and hit him over the head with her purse while the other parent yelled for security.

Joseph heard the commotion and made his way over to them.

Daniel saw Joseph coming and panicked. Daniel stomped on the woman's foot.

The woman screeched in pain and released Daniel's shirt.

Daniel ran off.

Joseph chased.

Two security guards approached the parents and tried to get the mother of the young boy that yelled, "stranger danger," to tell them what had happened, but she was in too much pain to speak.

The pain in her foot subsided, she described Daniel's shirt and pointed in the direction he ran.

"After him, before he gets away!" the other parent commanded.

The security guards ran off in search of a man fitting Daniel's description.

The women grabbed hold of their children and ran behind the two security guards to help with the search.

CHAPTER 7:

CATCH ME IF YOU CAN

Daniel ran into a nearby clothing store and hid behind a clothing rack in the center of the store. He watched as Joseph ran by.

"Do you need any help?" an assistant asked.

"Yes," said Daniel as he came out from the clothing rack and grabbed the nearest shirt within arm's reach. "I would like to purchase this."

On their way to the register, Daniel put on a large hat covering the top portion of his face. As soon as the cashier handed Daniel his purchase receipt he ripped the tags from each item then left the store.

Walking by Joseph, Daniel sighed in relief when he was not noticed.

"Daniel!" Joseph called out after noticing his shoes.

Daniel stiffened before running off accidentally bumping into an elderly lady, he caused her to shuffle into Joseph's way to slow him down.

"Oh dear," the lady cried out as she tried to balance herself. She called out to her son Stevie for help who was in the nearby store looking for games to play on his PlayStation Four console.

"Move it, lady," ordered Joseph as he ruthlessly shoved the woman to the side.

After witnessing the way Joseph handled his mother, Stevie ran out of the store after him.

Daniel made it to the end of the corridor, which turned out to be a dead end. He turned. His heart felt as if it plummeted to his stomach at the sight of Joseph, who was only a few feet in front of him.

Joseph stretched his hand forward to grab Daniel but when he was only inches away from gripping him by the shirt, a force unbeknownst to Joseph had stopped him.

Daniel looked over Joseph's shoulder. His eyes grew wide. He could not speak.

Joseph slowly turned his head to see someone else's hand holding his wrist. "Just who do-" Joseph was unable to finish his sentence. His mouth flopped open when he saw a giant of a man towering over him, with veins raging through his bulging muscles. Before Joseph could utter another word, the man punched him in the gut.

"This is for my mother," growled Stevie as he pounced on Joseph.

Joseph dropped to the floor in a fetal position to protect the most vulnerable parts of his body.

"You are a mean person," said Stevie. He kicked Joseph's backside. "And this is for making me chase after you!" Then Stevie ran to his mother weeping like a kid. "Mommy, are you okay?"

"What was all that about?" wheezed Joseph as he struggled to get up from the floor.

Meanwhile, at the other end of the hall, Daniel turned the corner and slowed down when he looked back and saw he was in the clear. He hunched over then pressed the back of his body against the wall to catch his breath. Daniel felt overheated and took off his sweater.

"Well, congratulations," an elderly woman stated as she ate her ice cream from a small cup using a long handle spoon.

"Congratulations for what?" asked Daniel.

"For winning the new car, silly," said the woman. She pointed at Daniel's pants pocket. "In the lobby of the food court. You should be more careful with that ticket hanging out like that. I'm surprised no one hasn't tried to steal it from you."

"So, this is what you were after," muttered Daniel.

"What?" asked the woman.

"Oh, nothing. Thank you," said Daniel.

"You're welcome," said the lady as she walked off dancing as she ate her ice cream.

Daniel grabbed the ticket and placed both hands in his pants pockets. Moments later Joseph turned the corner and ran into Daniel.

"Why did you run off so quick?" asked Joseph.

"I had something important to take care of and didn't want to interrupt you because you seemed to be enjoying yourself," improvised Daniel.

"Yes, I was. You didn't hear me calling you?" asked Joseph.

"No," answered Daniel.

"Don't worry about it. I got you, I mean, I'm caught up with you now," said Joseph.

"Would you like to get something to eat? I seemed to work up quite an appetite," said Daniel.

Joseph hesitated while looking around to see if he saw any billboards posting the winning ticket numbers.

"Um, sure," said Joseph.

Standing in line at the restaurant, Daniel heard a familiar laugh. He slithered the stems of a plant to the side. His body became paralyzed and he was unable to speak because of what he saw. He saw Karen sitting with an unknown man at the table. But once Daniel saw the man's watch he realized he was the same person from the night before.

"And what will you be having sir?" the cashier asked.

After the cashier's second attempt to get Daniel's attention to take his order, Joseph puckered his lips and looked at Daniel.

"Is everything okay?" asked Joseph.

"No. I'm not really in the mood to eat here. Can we just walk around the Mall for a bit?" asked Daniel.

Joseph, who could care less, went along with Daniel hoping to get his hands on that ticket. Walking by a clothing store Daniel, observed a mannequin wearing a similar shirt he had on earlier but with a different collar in the window.

"Nice. Let's go in here. Looks like they got some really cool clothes," said Daniel.

"I don't know," hesitated Joseph.

Daniel refused to take no for an answer and entered the store. Joseph reluctantly followed a few paces behind. They made their way to the men's department where Daniel tapped a sales associate on the shoulder.

"Hello. Can you tell me where I could find the shirt in the window?" asked Daniel.

"Yes. It's over there to the left in the men's section near the restroom," said the sales associate. She pointed without raising her head.

"Where's the restroom?" Daniel asked.

"Follow me," sighed the sales associate.

Daniel had to run to keep up with her. She walked very fast. As Joseph and Daniel followed the sale's associate, Joseph grabbed a few other shirts from off the clothing rack.

"This is it. I have to buy this shirt for you," said Daniel.

"No, you don't," replied Joseph as he tried to hide the shirts he grabbed from off the rack behind his back.

"It's the least I could do for all you've done for me," insisted Daniel.

"Trust me. You don't have to buy THAT shirt," said Joseph.

Joseph continued to insist that Daniel not purchase the shirt but Daniel would not let up. Joseph finally agreed and accepted Daniel's gesture after he saw Daniel was on the edge of becoming annoyed. On the way to the dressing room, he daydreamed of himself tossing the shirt out of the window of the new car as he drove off.

Daniel browsed through the store as he waited for Joseph to try on the shirt. He saw a poster of a male model modeling a designer's outfit and stopped another sales associate walking by.

"Excuse me, Jennie, I want to look just like that," declared Daniel as he pointed at the poster.

Jennie took a step back to look him over. "Honey, I'm a sales associate, not a plastic surgeon, but I'll try my best." She turned around clearing her throat and yells, "Team," waving a white cloth.

Two flamboyant males dashed over to them.

"Girl, I thought you'd never call," one of the associates responded.

"Ooh honey when these hands get finished with you, you are going to be fabulous!" the other associate exclaimed.

"This is my team. This is the lovely Keona and dynamic Dana. Team, this is, um… I'm sorry. Your name. What is your name, sir?" asked Jennie.

"Daniel."

"Daniel. That's nice. Okay team, Daniel, follow me," ordered Jennie.

Daniel hesitated but followed with an alarmed look on his face. Jennie marched to the other end of the men's section with Keona and Dana following closely behind her. Jennie suddenly stopped and faced

Daniel. Keona and Dana stopped and faced each other as Daniel walked through them toward Jennie.

"Don't be scared," whispered Dana.

"She won't bite," uttered Keona.

"But I might," said Dana in a deep manly tone as he smiled flirtatiously at Daniel.

Jennie handed Daniel several outfits to try on. He exited the dressing room after trying on the first outfit.

"No, no, no," repeated Dana. He waved his hands and shook his head as he rejected all of the outfits Daniel tried on.

"What's wrong? I like this one," replied Daniel as he examined himself in the mirror.

"Of course, you would," said Dana.

"Please take it off," begged Keona. "That outfit makes you look like my third-grade teacher."

"No. I mean, the clothes are great. They just don't fit you," said Keona when Daniel exited the dressing room after trying on the next outfit.

"I need to call heaven." Dana pulled out her cell phone. "They said a Divine intervention is on its way." Dana and Keona laughed.

"This is worse than I expected," uttered Jennie. She threw her head into her lap. "I got it." She got up and ran around the store. She grabbed a variety of garments from different racks. She tossed the outfits at Daniel and shoved him into the dressing room. "This is going to be a life changer, definitely."

"Okay. I'm coming out," yelled Daniel a few minutes later from behind the curtains.

Jennie, Keona, and Dana nearly fainted when Daniel walked out of the dressing room.

"So, what do you all think?" asked Daniel nervously.

"I did it! I did it!" said Jennie with excitement as she jumped up and down while holding onto Dana's arm.

"Don't you mean, *we* did it?" interjected Keona while he swooped back his invisible long flowing hair.

"I know, right," said Dana as he and Keona walked off. "Like she was over here by herself helping him this whole time."

Daniel walked in front of the mirror and looked himself over in wonder. "Boy, clothes sure do make a difference."

"No, clothes just help. It's you that makes the difference, once you make them," Jennie replied, in a surprising display of frankness. "Now go ahead and walk. Show me what you got."

Daniel sucked in his stomach, puffed out his chest and took a few steps down the aisle of the store, becoming distracted by women gawking at him. He tripped over his own foot, fell to the floor, and quickly picked himself up. He walked over to Jennie saying, "I'll take everything I have on plus whatever my friend is getting."

Jennie smiled and walked off. Joseph exited the dressing room.

"Look at you," said Joseph then looked in the mirror and said, "Look at me."

"Do you think Karen will like the new look?" asked Daniel.

"I do," said Joseph.

"You don't look bad yourself. Love that shirt," said Daniel after looking Joseph over.

On their way to the register, Joseph tried to talk Daniel out of buying the shirt for him. But Daniel insisted.

"This is a gift from me to you. Something I want you to remember me by," said Daniel knowing Joseph could not say no to getting the shirt after that.

"I could think of other ways to remember you by," Joseph said in an undertone.

Outside of the store, Daniel stopped, bringing a tear to his eye with some effort. "Joseph, it would mean a lot to me if you wear the shirt."

"What shirt?" asked Joseph blankly.

"The one I just bought for you," said Daniel.

"Oh, *that* shirt," said Joseph. He knew exactly what shirt Daniel was speaking of. He just hoped Daniel would have forgotten about it.

"Yes, that shirt," said Daniel.

"You mean now? You want me to put on the shirt right now," said Joseph.

"Yes, I do," smiled Daniel.

"I'm already wearing clothes," protested Joseph. He pointed to himself.

"But the shirt matches your pants. How much would it hurt for you to wear the shirt purchased by your new friend?" asked Daniel then softly grinned.

"Why not," said Joseph with a forced smile. "After all, we are friends."

Daniel's heart had started to soften. He began to view Joseph as a possible friend and thought about telling him to take off the shirt but hesitated.

"Since we're bonding, I want to let you in on something," said Joseph as he forced his head through the collar of the shirt.

"And what's that?" asked Daniel.

"I want to let you in on how I occasionally spend my days to kill some time. Follow me." Joseph walked off with a devilish smirk, his eyes focused on what was ahead.

"Okay," said Daniel as he followed Joseph. He wanted to have an opened mind, but did not know what to expect. He curiously walked beside Joseph as they entered a lingerie store.

"You see; the thing is not to use the same girl more than once in the same week or month," whispered Joseph while leaning into Daniel.

"And why is this?" asked Daniel. He was confused by Joseph's statement.

"Because you don't want to be remembered by any of the ladies," answered Joseph.

Daniel was still unsure of what Joseph was talking about, so he carefully observed Joseph as he walked around the store.

"Hi. My name is Megan," a sales associate said she reached her hand out to shake Joseph's hand.

He pretended to be embarrassed to be in the store. "Yes. I have been in a relationship for quite some time, and I would like to get my significant other something nice."

"Oh, how sweet," replied Megan as her face light up with joy. "So how long have you two been dating?" she asked pointing at Daniel.

"Oh no, no, no," replied Daniel.

"No, he's just a friend. My significant other is indeed a woman. Her name is Sharon," improvised Joseph.

"Sharon, lovely," said Megan. She walked them around the store to show them the collection of perfumes he could purchase. But no matter what item she showed Joseph nothing would do.

"Perfumes are great, but she really has more than she needs," said Joseph.

"Well let's go over here to our lovely lingerie collection," said Megan.

"Okay," said Joseph.

"No, no. None of these really speak to me, you know," said Joseph after Megan showed him a few pieces of lingerie.

"Yes, I do. You know a shipment came in earlier, and I know there are some pieces in the back I'm sure she'll love. I will be right back," said Megan as she walked to the back room of the store that was behind the counter.

"This is going to be fun," said Joseph as he turned to Daniel while he rubbed his hands together and nodded his head.

Megan came from the back with a variety of pieces in different sizes. "Do you know her measurements?"

"Measurements?" asked Joseph.

"Yes, measurements," replied Megan. She moved her hand over her breast to let Joseph know she was asking about his girlfriend's cup size.

"Oh, size. No, I don't. I hate to ask, but would you mind trying one on seeing that you look about the same size as her and all?" asked Joseph. He could see from Megan's facial expression she was becoming disturbed by the question. "I understand if you don't want to, having a belly and all," he uttered in a nonchalant tone to distract her, which seemed to work.

"My belly," said Megan.

"It is a bit on the puffy side," said Joseph.

"Excuse you, but there is nothing wrong with my belly," snapped Megan.

"Okay. If you say so," said Joseph.

"Give me the lingerie. I'll show you," huffed Megan.

"I can't believe what I'm seeing," said Daniel. He grabbed Joseph by the collar and forced him out of the store shoving him against the wall. "I cannot believe you. Just when I was starting to like you, you go and pull this."

"What, it's not like I was making her do something she did not want to. What's the big deal?" asked Joseph.

"You-" Before Daniel could say another word, the security guards and the two angry parents with their kids surrounded Daniel and Joseph.

"There he is!" shouted the woman in an angry tone whose foot Daniel stomped on earlier.

"No, wait," said Daniel. He squinted and held out his hands as one of the security guards approached them. The security guards pulled out their handcuffs. Daniel shivered at the sound of metal clinching together.

"I got him into custody," said one of the security guards.

Joseph became perplexed. Daniel slowly opened his eyes in surprise. The security guard put the handcuffs on Joseph instead of Daniel.

"I think there's been a mistake," cried Joseph.

"There's no mistake," cried one of the parents. "He's still wearing that same ugly shirt. You ought to arrest him just for that."

At that very instance, Joseph knew it was Daniel who was behind him getting arrested and the real reason Daniel was so insistent on buying him that shirt. However, Joseph was more amused than upset that Daniel pulled off such a deceitful scheme to have him arrested and take possession of the car without him realizing what was happening.

"You know, I didn't even see it coming," said Joseph admiringly. He smiled as the security guards dragged him off.

Joseph was arrested and awaiting trial. He was charged with attempted kidnapping of a minor. The fact that he had prior warrants in other states did not help him much at all.

Daniel casually walked back to work twirling the keys to his new car around his finger. Just as he entered the workplace, he received a text from Karen that read, "Loved lunch. Can't wait to do it again soon."

I might just have a chance, after all, Daniel thought. He walked over to everyone who was circled around Mr. Jameson. "What's going on?" he whispered to a coworker named Kyle.

"Mr. Jameson is about to announce the person selected for the new management position," said Kyle excitedly.

"Okay everyone, I'm not going to keep you long," said Mr. Jameson as he pulled out an envelope from his inside jacket pocket. "The lucky victim, I mean, the lucky person is... What? Daniel." Everyone was just as shocked as Mr. Jameson, but not more than Daniel that Mr. Jameson said his name. "Congratulations Daniel," Mr. Jameson complimented him and shook his hand. "I hope you are not upset by what I said the other day."

"Don't worry about it," said Daniel.

Mr. Jameson handed Daniel a fancy invitation to meet Mr. Cedar, the Chief Executive Officer and owner of the company at Ruth's Chris Steak House. The invitation read to be there at seven.

"Go home and rest for tonight. You'll need it," said Mr. Jameson.

On his way home, Daniel's cheeks flushed. He could not stop smiling as his heart raced because of his new position on the job and receiving the new car. Then he thought what it all could mean for him becoming Karen's new boss. And just like that, his celebration was over. Reality struck, and boy did it suck.

CHAPTER 8:

THE BAIT & SWITCH

Six o'clock came sooner than expected, and Daniel had been pacing back and forth in his living room for the past hour and a half. "Ugh, what should I do?" He stopped in the center of the room. "Oh - I got it."

Daniel grabbed a writing pad and searched the apartment for a pen. He had dozens of pens placed throughout the apartment. But as always, there was not one to be found when he really needed one. He finally found one and drew a line down the center. He labeled one column Love and the other Career.

Starting with the Love column he wrote "wife," "companion," and "family." In the Career column, he wrote "money to do" and drew an arrow to the Love column then wrote beneath that "No Karen." Insecurity and defeat swept over him. He stood in front of the mirror thinking about everything that took place between him, Karen, Mr. Jameson, and his coworkers.

"Maybe Karen will compromise. I'll just ask her to go work at a different store." Realizing how foolish it would be for him to ask such a thing he freshened up and went to the restaurant to announce his decision that may be the start of a new career or the ending of a relationship that had barely begun.

Daniel drove up to the restaurant and exited the car, handing his keys to the valet attendant. "Take care of her. She's new."

On his way into the restaurant, he collected his thoughts and quickly rehearsed what he was going to say. After pulling himself together he walked up to the hostess.

"Will you be dining alone?" said the hostess.

"No. My name is Daniel, I'm looking for Mr. Cedar."

"Yes, Mr. Cedar, he's been expecting you," said the hostess. She grabbed a menu and silverware, and said, "Right this way."

As Daniel followed the hostess he cleared his throat and prepared himself to announce his decision.

"Are we expecting someone else?" asked Daniel as he looked at the empty seat next to him.

"Yes," answered Mr. Cedar as he raised his hand to signal for the waitress to come to him.

Daniel's eyes took hold of Mr. Cedar's watch, and to his surprise, it was the same watch the man was wearing with the distinctive scar above the wristband who was dining out with Karen the other night. "You disgusting pig!" shouted Daniel in an uncontrollable rage.

"Excuse me?" said Mr. Cedar as he arched his brows.

Mr. Jameson tried to control the situation and calm everyone down. He then pleaded with Daniel to control his anger by reminding him of the purpose of the dinner. However, Daniel refused and told Mr. Cedar he could never work for someone like him.

"You have just made my decision easier," proclaimed Daniel.

"Now, you just wait a minute," barked Mr. Cedar. He pounded his fist on the table. "Mr. Jameson, just what type of crew are you running over there with employees behaving like this?"

"I am just as perplexed as you Mr. Cedar. I have never seen him behave like this before," said Mr. Jameson. He then turned to Daniel and hissed, "What has gotten into you?"

Daniel, with confidence in his decision, stood tall and held his shoulders back. "I will tell you exactly what has gotten into me... Karen."

"What is going on?" asked Karen as she walked up to the table.

"Wait. What are you doing here?" asked Daniel. He was lost and confused.

"These are my parents," exclaimed Karen.

"I don't understand," said Daniel.

"I took a different last name to hide my identity. I didn't want anyone to know who I was. I've been working for the company as an intern to gain experience before working at a different company," said Karen.

"A different company," said Daniel blankly.

"Yes, but right here in town," said Karen.

"I feel so foolish right now," muttered Daniel, and blushing hard informed everyone for the reason behind his outburst.

After a brief awkward moment of silence, they all burst into laughter. Daniel was just glad at how understanding everyone was. Especially Mr. Cedar and Karen, and how he was going to keep his job.

After dinner, Karen told her parents she was going to stay behind with Daniel and take a taxi home. She took hold of Daniel's arm as he led her outside of the restaurant.

"It sure is a lovely night tonight. Would you like to go for a walk?" asked Daniel.

Karen agreed. She stopped Daniel and looked him in the eye. "So, tell me, how was your day?"

"Other than me escaping from my stalker, winning a new car, getting a promotion, and going on a date with you, it was pretty normal," said Daniel dryly.

Karen's level of interest was elevated. "You have to tell me all about that."

"Another time. I can't help but worry, your mother must think I'm awful," said Daniel.

"No. Surprisingly, she doesn't," said Karen.

The valet drove up in Daniel's car.

"This is her," said Daniel proudly.

"She's beautiful," admired Karen.

"She sure is," said Daniel while he looked to Karen.

Karen smiled when she saw Daniel was looking at her and not the car. "Tell me. Where's the first place you'd like to go in your new car?"

"Get in and I'll show you," said Daniel after giving it some thought.

"Right now?" asked Karen.

"Yes, but I need to make one stop before we go," said Daniel.

The two hopped into the car and Daniel drove back to his apartment. Charlie and Benny were sitting on the porch drinking beer.

"I can't believe she dumped me," Bennie whined to Charlie while looking through pictures of his girlfriend on his phone.

"Hello," said Daniel as he got out of the car. He ran into the apartment.

"Was that your roommate?" Bennie asked Charlie.

"I think it was," Charlie responded in shock.

In the apartment, Daniel grabbed a midsize envelope from off his bed and stopped when he looked in the mirror and saw himself. It was as if he saw himself for the first time. At that moment he realized his life had changed. He had changed. He was not the same person standing in the parking lot speaking with his parents months earlier, and he was okay with it. He smiled and left the apartment.

In the car, Daniel adjusted his seat and the mirrors before driving off.

"No, no. Seatbelt," said Karen.

Daniel laughed and said, "Oh yes. I'm going to have to get used to that."

Driving onto the highway he gazed at Karen's beauty as he drove down the freeway. After some hours passed, Karen awakened as the sun hit her face.

"Good morning beautiful," said Daniel to her while moving her hair out of her face.

"Good morning. Have you been driving all night?" asked Karen.

"Yes. I did stop a few times for gas," said Daniel.

"Where are we going?" asked Karen.

"You'll see when we get there," said Daniel.

After getting off the freeway and turning a few corners, Karen became alarmed when she noticed Daniel was pulling up to a correctional facility.

He must be lost. Karen bit her fingernails. "Are you stopping to ask for directions?"

"No," said Daniel as he parked the car and turned the engine off.

Her heart skipped a bit. She nervously hopped out of the car watching two officers walk their dogs as they sniff around the outer fence in the parking lot.

"After this, we'll take a break and get the cars," said one of the officers told his partner.

Karen tightly gripped Daniel's arm. "Usually when a guy is ready for me to meet someone he doesn't take me to a prison."

Daniel and Karen checked into the facility and sat at a designated table in the visiting room when called. Karen became frightened when the bell rang accompanied with the squeaky sound from the rusted door opening. She moved closer to Daniel as the prisoners were brought from the back. Daniel was surprised that another one of the prisoners was Rusty from the bar. He avoided making eye contact with Rusty, he did not want Karen to know he knew him too.

Joseph entered the room, smiled when he saw Daniel and sat down at their table.

"Hello, Joseph," said Daniel.

"Daniel, I'm surprised to see you here," said Joseph.

"Yes. And this is-"

"Karen. Yes, I know who she is," said Joseph.

"He does?" whispered Karen when she leaned into Daniel.

Daniel laughed and said to Joseph, "I just thought it would be fitting for me to visit you since you played a major part in where I'm at now, and with whom."

"Well, I could say the same about you, except the visiting part."

"Before I go, I brought you a gift," said Daniel.

"Visiting time is over," announced a guard.

Daniel quickly handed Joseph the envelope he grabbed from off his bed. The bell rang for the visitors to leave and the prisoners to return to their cells.

The guard spoke into his walkie-talkie and requested for Joseph's cell door to be shut.

Joseph sat on his bed, opened the envelope, and pulled out the card. Joseph smiled and laughed hysterically after opening the card. Inside the card was a photo of Daniel holding the keys to the car surrounded by people holding balloons and a cake that read "congratulations."

You see, when Joseph turned the corner and ran up to Daniel after getting beat up by Stevie, Daniel was putting the keys to the car in his pocket, not the ticket. He used that time to turn in his ticket and run back to that location to wait for Joseph to arrive to put his plan for getting the security guards to mistake his identity for Joseph in motion.

"Good for you Daniel. Good for you," smiled Joseph as he taped the photo on the wall next to his bed.

As for Daniel and Karen, their story is still in the making.

TO BE

CONTNUED...

www.ingramcontent.com/pod-product-compliance
Lightning Source LLC
Chambersburg PA
CBHW070801120626
46557CB00002B/680